11:33
10/0

Iris VanRynbach

Cecily's Christmas

⊞ Greenwillow Books, New York

Watercolor paints and
a pen line were used
for the full-color art.
The text type
is ITC Garamond.

Printed in Singapore
by Tien Wah Press
First Edition
10 9 8 7 6 5 4 3 2 1

Library of Congress
Cataloging-in-Publication Data

VanRynbach, Iris.
Cecily's Christmas /
by Iris VanRynbach.
p.   cm.
Summary:
Cecily does not seem as
interested in the Christmas
preparations as her
sister Amelie, until
the big day arrives.
ISBN 0-688-07832-X.
ISBN 0-688-07833-8 (lib. bdg.)
[1. Christmas—Fiction.
2. Sisters—Fiction.]
I. Title.
PZ7.V354Ce   1988
[E]—dc19
87-34083   CIP   AC

E
Y

FOR AMÉLIE

AND CECILY,

AND MY SISTER ANGELA

Amelie and her mother
and father picked out
a Christmas tree.

Cecily wanted the
Christmas tree sign.

Amelie and her mother and
father decorated the tree.

Cecily hung the ornaments
on Suzie.

Amelie was an angel
in the school play.

Cecily sang Jingle Bells
in the audience.

Amelie and her mother
made Christmas cookies.

Cecily ate them.

Amelie and Cecily went
to visit Santa Claus.
Amelie talked to Santa.

SANTA
10 - 4

Cecily just wanted
to ride the reindeer.

Amelie and her mother wrapped the Christmas presents.

Cecily got tangled up
in ribbon and tape.

Amelie and her parents hung
their stockings over the
fireplace on Christmas Eve.

Cecily tried to wear hers.

But on Christmas morning
Cecily was the first one up—and
she brought presents to everyone!
"Merry Christmas," she said.